With very best regards from

Wendy Watson

For Lou-Lou

BY
CLYDE
WATSON

TOM FOX
And the Apple Pie

ILLUSTRATED BY
WENDY
WATSON

THOMAS Y. CROWELL COMPANY   NEW YORK

Books by Clyde and Wendy Watson

FATHER FOX'S PENNYRHYMES

TOM FOX AND THE APPLE PIE

Designed by Wendy Watson

Manufactured in the United States of America

L.C. Card 74-171010
ISBN 0-690-82783-0   0-690-82784-9 (LB)

1 2 3 4 5 6 7 8 9 10

Down at the end of Mulberry Lane, there once lived a family of red foxes. There was Pa Fox and Ma Fox and fourteen little red foxes, all the way down to Tom Fox. (Here is a secret you mustn't pass on: Tom Fox was the greediest and laziest little fox in the family. But he was also the youngest and sweetest, as is so often the case.)

One fine summer morning, Tom Fox woke up early and opened the window to let the sun come in. He poked his nose out the window, and then climbed onto the sill, for the smell of something very sweet was blowing in the wind.

"Apple pie!" he said to himself. "That's what it is!" And he looked toward the village, for the wind came from there. In the distance he could see crazy kites and bright balloons flying high above treetips and rooftops.

He pricked up his ears and heard the faraway sounds of music and dancing and laughter.

"Hey!" he shouted. "Hallo! Help! The Fair is here!"

His thirteen brothers and sisters woke up and they started to shout too.

"The Fair! Whoopee! The Fair is here!"

Tom Fox and his special sister Lou-Lou ran to the hollow tree and pulled out their bag of pennies. Tom tied it to his belt.

"I want a big blue balloon," said Lou-Lou.

"You know what I want?" asked Tom.

But just at that moment, Ma and Pa Fox appeared.

"Breakfast!" said Ma Fox. "Cornbread and Honey!"

"And then out to the garden," said Pa Fox. "There's work to be done."

But didn't I tell you little Tom Fox was the laziest and greediest fox child of all? Besides, there was nothing he loved better than apple pie. So along about noon, he whispered good-bye to Lou-Lou, sneaked away through the rows of corn, and set off for town sniffing the wind and following his nose.

He hadn't far to go before he saw the striped tops of tents, and the music got louder, the colors brighter, the smells more delicious, and then—

there he was in the middle of the fairgrounds. All around him were candy booths and pop-corn booths, booths where you could buy apples and cider, ginger cookies and lollipops, to say nothing of booths where you could try your skill and win all sorts of grand prizes....But Tom Fox knew what he wanted, and he headed straight for the apple pie booth.

There he saw tiny apple pies as small as a paw, and big enormous pies the size of Lou-Lou, but Tom settled for a splendid middle-sized pie all brown and crisp and juicy. He counted out twenty-five pennies and the pie lady tied the pie all up in a box. With his last five pennies Tom got a great big blue balloon with a face on it for Lou-Lou. And then, with the box under his arm and the balloon tied to his belt, Tom started off home, hoping to get there before anyone noticed he was gone.

As he walked, he could just see Ma Fox's knife slicing the pie into sixteen pieces, one for everybody, and he hurried even faster toward home. But suddenly he slowed down.

"Feathers and Foxgloves!" he said out loud. "If this poor pie is cut into sixteen pieces, how tiny those pieces will be! Why, they'll be so small, I won't taste the apple part at all!" So he thought. And this is what he came up with:

"But," he thought as he rounded a bend, "The pieces still won't be all <u>that</u> big. Why not stay awake until the others fall asleep, and then Lou-Lou and I will sneak out of bed and tiptoe downstairs with the pie and surprise Ma and Pa! That's only four of us, and four big pieces of pie!"

He stuck his nose in the box. Um-m-m! If only Lou-Lou were there! The two of them could share it, and each take half.

Just then a brown toad hopped across the road.

"What a pity to cut it at all," muttered the toad as he disappeared on the other side.

"Of course!" said Tom. He sat down under the hedge and opened the box, and do you know what?

He ate the WHOLE PIE all by himself.

He was so full when he finished the last bite that he fell fast asleep under the hedge. When he woke up it was dark, and the moon was rising. Now they'd know he was gone for sure! Oh, No!

He ran on home, and puffed in at the door. There sat the whole fox family just finishing a grand supper of beans and carrots fresh from the garden, and not a snip of a bean nor the end of a carrot was left for Tom.

"To bed without your supper, you lazy child!" said Ma Fox.

But did Tom Fox care? No sir! His stomach
was warm and full with eating
that fine apple
pie.

Clyde Watson

is an educator and a musician, as well as an author. She majored in music at Smith College and after her graduation played the violin professionally with orchestras. But a stint of teaching young children led her to a growing interest in innovative techniques, and she decided to study for a Ph.D. in education. She now lives on an Indian reservation in Maine, where she has been teaching in an elementary school for Passamaquoddy and Penobscot children and working on a project to develop bilingual learning materials for Indian children. Besides this book, she has also written *Father Fox's Pennyrhymes* and several other books for children, all illustrated by her sister Wendy.

Wendy Watson

has won many prizes and awards for her spirited and distinctive illustrations. A graduate of Bryn Mawr College, Wendy Watson now lives in the heart of New York City, but her illustrations usually reflect her happy memories of growing up in a large family in rural Vermont. The pictures for *Tom Fox and the Apple Pie*, executed in black-and-white on scratchboard with an overlay of color on acetate, are filled with affectionate and humorous references to small-town American life.